TABULETTA

Kimberly Moses

REJOICE
Essential Publishing

Kimberly Moses/Rejoice Essential Publishing

PO BOX 512

Effingham, SC 29541

www.republishing.org

Unless otherwise indicated, scripture is taken from the King James Version.'

Tabuletta/Kimberly Moses

ISBN-13: 978-1-956775-10-5

Library of Congress Control: 2021952120

CONTENTS

PREFACE

Dreams are so important and many people dismiss them. When they wake up in the morning, they go about their day, never writing down what they dreamt. God speaks to us in dreams and He gives us wonderful ideas. It is up to us to pursue what was in our dreams. If I had never written down my dream on a note app on my phone, you would not be reading this book. I could not shake this dream, and I knew in my heart that I had to explore it to see where it would lead me. Since I'm an author of forty-plus books, I was excited to expound on the dream and make it into a book and a film later. I am ecstatic to write more Tabuletta series soon.

CHAPTER 1

THINGS JUST GOT STRANGE

Jane Walker was an attractive girl trying to get on her feet. She was often misunderstood due to her sarcastic personality. She tried modeling but was told that she was too short. She tried her hand at many jobs but faced rejection, discrimination, and unjust practices. She was underpaid but stayed on various jobs in order to survive in New York City. The cost of living there was expensive but after many months of hardship, some of the pressure of life was lifted when she moved in with her boyfriend Josh. They met at a Turkish restaurant where she was hostess and Josh was a line cook. Jane would often have time to meet with Josh when picking up an order from the kitchen.

Jane and Josh noticed each other one Saturday night when the restaurant was extremely busy. Immediately there was an attraction but there was no time for talking because orders were coming in constantly. The restaurant was on an hour wait for people to dine in. When the shift was over, Jane felt like she could finally breathe. As she went into the back to gather her bag, Josh was there putting on his jacket. He turned around and greeted her.

"Hello," he said.

"Hey," Jane replied.

"We survived," Josh said through a shy chuckle.

"Yeah. I can now breathe and get back to my life now that it's over," Jane said in her own sarcastic humor.

Josh laughed then asked, "Are you driving, catching a cab, or walking?"

"Does it look like this girl drives?" she remarked.

Josh was a bit taken back but then Jane smiled. He then realized she was joking.

"Hmm. Okay. You are a jokester," he laughed nervously.

"Sorry for messing around. Yes, I like to put people on the spot. To answer your question, I am walking," she responded.

"Ok, well let me walk you home," he insisted.

"Ok, cool -Thank you," Jane said.

Josh and Jane walked the streets of New York City. It was around 11:30 pm. They laughed and talked the whole time. As they approached Jane's building, she stopped.

"Okay. This is me," she said.

"I would like to walk you home more often. Can I have your number?" he asked.

"Yes, I'd like that," Jane said. Josh took out his cellphone and Jane grabbed it. She entered her number, called herself, and gave the phone back.

"I'll save it. Good night," he said.

"You better save it. Good night" Jane said feisty-like.

Josh kept walking and Jane went inside of her building. She took the elevator up to the third floor, and walked into her apartment. Suddenly thoughts of Josh flooded her mind and her face lit up.

Every night, Josh and Jane got to know each other as he walked her home after the shifts. The two eventually started dating. Josh decided to leave the Turkish restaurant to start collecting trash because it paid more money. Josh and Jane were happy and wanted to take their relationship to the next level. One day Josh asked Jane to move in with him. Jane was ecstatic and agreed.

Weeks passed and one morning during breakfast Jane picked up the newspaper that sat on the table. The headlines read: "Mysterious Lab Fire." As she proceeded to read the article, Josh walked into the kitchen and kissed her on her cheek.

"Hey babe," he said as he sat down.

"Hey you," Jane replied.

"What are you reading," he asked.

"Scientists are trying to determine how this lab downtown caught on fire," she replied.

"Oh okay. I think I'll just have a bagel and coffee this morning. Something light. I am going to do some tidying around here on my day off," Josh stated.

"That's good. I'm going to work today. They need the extra help right now," Jane replied.

"Okay. I will be here, waiting for you my love, when you get back," Josh smiled and went over to the counter to finish making his breakfast.

Jane got up from the table, walked over to Josh, kissed him, then headed out the door to work. As she walked several blocks to work, the thoughts about the mysterious lab fire played in her mind.

"It seems so weird. I wonder what caused it. Maybe I should walk past the building to see how it looks."

Jane decided not to go to work that day. She decided to surprise Josh and pick up some Chinese takeout. The plan was to come home and spend time with him for his day off. She had been working overtime to pay off some credit card debt she accumulated during the time when finding a job was scarce. She wanted financial freedom so she and Josh could marry and start a family. She didn't want to put her baggage on him.

Jane knew where the lab was located so she walked past it on her way to work. She stared into the dark abandoned building. There was a fence barricade to prevent trespassing that was set up on the side of the building but Jane squeezed through one of the openings. She could smell the fire and as she walked closer to the building, her tongue tasted aluminum, boride, and chromium.

"That's weird," she said out loud and smacked while tasting the air. "Why do I know how various elements taste and why am I drawn here? This is stupid. I need to get out of here before I get caught."

Jane was overwhelmed by a pulling urge to investigate the fire. She stepped past the caution tape and examined the surroundings. She saw the shattered glass, the black soot, ashes of the once top of the line equipment, burned binders and cabinets. She knew immediately that the reason for the explosion had to do with radioactive material.

"Oh my goodness! How do I know this? What is going on with me?"

Immediately, her body started reacting to her surroundings, and her eyes began to glow green and her skin darkened into a pale greyish lead-like tone. She looked at her arms, hands and felt them. "Oh no. They are made of lead," she shrieked.

She panicked and rushed out of the building. As she dashed off, she went behind a building out of view because she didn't want anyone to see her. She found a brick wall to lean against so she could catch her breath and collect her thoughts. After a few deep breaths, she held up her arms and hands and they were normal.

"Wow. I don't know what is going on with me. I better get home and relax. Josh and I can go get dinner later."

Jane walked several blocks home and entered her building. As she got closer to her apartment, she heard moans coming from the other side of the door. She knew someone was having sex but it didn't register with her that it could be Josh.

"Josh wouldn't cheat on me. He loves me," she thought.

Jane quickly stuck the key into the door and rushed in to see what was occurring. To her surprise, Josh was having sex with someone else. He was on top of a brunette. Jane froze in disbelief and dropped her bag. When Josh and the brunette heard her, they were frightened and stopped. They hurriedly gathered covers from the bed to hide their nakedness.

"Get out!" Jane yelled at the brunette. The lady grabbed the sheet, rushed to the living room, got her belongings and left the apartment. She finished dressing as she ran down the hall.

"Babe, it's not what it seems," Josh tried to explain as he sat up in bed trying to get dressed.

"Not what it seems? You must think I'm stupid! You were having sex with someone else!" Jane shouted angrily.

"Babe, it meant nothing. It's you that I want. I'm sorry. Please forgive me," Josh pleaded.

"Forgive you? We are done! So this is what you have been doing when I'm away," Jane said while rolling her eyes in disgust.

"No. It just happened. You are never here. You work all the time," Josh reached for excuses to explain his actions.

"So that's an excuse to cheat. I was working for us but now that's over," Jane said, picking up her bag, and heading towards the door.

"Baby, baby, hold on a minute. Don't leave," Josh said as he tried to embrace Jane.

"Get your hands off me. Don't ever touch me again. I'm moving out and never speaking to you again." Jane said as she pushed Josh's hands off her. She turned around and slammed the door.

As soon as she left, nausea hit her stomach and a dull pain shot through her heart. Jane had nowhere to go and she really didn't have a plan B. Building a future with Josh was her only plan. She felt the weight of her decision immediately.

"How could I be so stupid? Why didn't I see any red flags? How could he do this to me?" Jane's mind raced and tears streamed down her eyes. She walked until she came to the park. She needed to sit down somewhere and figure out her next steps. Before she could find a bench, a man approached her. He looked homeless. He wore a long dirty tannish trench coat, a black fedora hat, and a black scarf that covered all of his face except his eyes. As he got closer, Jane smelt chemicals but she was so focused on Josh's betrayal that she didn't have time to figure out where the smell was coming from. The mysterious man handed her a note with 7,000 in cash in an envelope. The address listed on the note was 511 Park Avenue.

"Help me and this money is yours," the man stressed.

"No, thank you," Jane said and walked away before the man could say anything else.

"That is so weird. The money probably has some strings attached. It's probably stolen. How does someone who looks like that have that sort of money? I don't know what kind of scam, kidnapping, or sex parade this man is running, but I won't be a part of it," Jane thought.

Finally Jane found a bench, she was looking forward to resting. She had enough drama for the day. While she tried to collect herself, she kept noticing the bummy looking man. He kept approaching people in the park, handing them the same note and envelope that she had refused. Next, the man approached a young college student and handed her the note with the envelope full of cash. She was reading a book for her class and the man said, "All you have to do is help me and the money is yours."

"Okay," she said while rolling her eyes. She took a hundred dollar bill from the envelope, shoved the envelope and note back to the man, took her book and proceeded to walk away.

It seemed her flippant disregard and dismissive actions infuriated the man and suddenly he looked up to the sky. Lightning started and the sky darkened. A surge of powerful green electricity pulsated through the man's body. This sight alarmed everyone in the park and they began to run away in fear.

"Uggh!" he yelled out in fury.

As he raised his arms, everyone fell to the ground in a paralytic state. They couldn't move. Everyone fell, that is, except Jane, she hid behind the bench for safety and to see what was going on. The man didn't notice her as he sent this strange power through everyone in the park. The longer he released this power, pills started to appear on the surface of the people's skin.

Every capsule, medicine, electrolyte, or ingested pill inside of them bubbled underneath their skin, burst through, hovered over their bodies, and moved towards the man.

Jane was terrified and held her breath so she wouldn't get caught. She put her hand over her mouth to ensure she didn't make any sounds.

The man opened up his jacket and all the pills gathered inside his inner pocket. The man dashed off into the night.

A few minutes went by and Jane came out of hiding. She was shunned to see so many bodies on the ground. No one was moving. They were all paralyzed. She walked over to a young man, and noticed that his eyes were wide open and he was conscious of his surroundings. However he couldn't speak when he tried to ask for help. Everyone in the park laid flat on their backs.

"Oh no," Jane said as she put her hands on her head. "Why wasn't I affected? It must have something to do with what happened to me earlier at the lab. Am I some kind of superhero with some super power? Am I called to stop this man?"

Jane picks up her phone and dials 911 for the massive crowd of frozen bodies.

CHAPTER 2

VENGEANCE ARISING

Jane sat in the interrogation room at the city police department.

"What did you see?" an older male detective asked.

"There was a bummy man dressed in a dirty trench coat wearing a fedora. He handed everyone he passed by a note with the address 511 Parker Avenue and included seven thousand dollars. He got upset when someone took some of his money. Then a green energy shot out of him paralyzing everyone around and pills started popping coming out of people's bodies," Jane explained.

The detective erupted in laughter. Apparently, this was an unbelievable story.

"I'm sorry but that is quite a story. You want me to believe a man with strange power paralyzed everyone and pills came out of them?" he asked.

"Yes, that's exactly what I want you to believe," Jane replied. She grew frustrated and felt like having this conversation was starting to become a waste of time.

"Well how come you weren't paralyzed?" the detective mocked.

"I don't know," Jane stated.

"Ok, we are done here. Please contact me if you have any more stories," the detective said.

Jane got up from the table, and walked out of the door. Once she was outside the police station she realized that she had nowhere to go. She regretted going to the police station because she knew the detective thought she was a laughing stock. Going back to the apartment she shared with Josh was not an option. Besides a few hours ago, he was screwing someone else!

"I'll know what I'll do. I will go to my job and sleep in the manager's office. However, I will have to sneak in and hide until everyone goes home," she thought.

Jane proceeded to walk to her job and when she got closer, she noticed that they were about to close up. This was her chance to sneak in and hide out in the bathroom. No one would go there since it was usually cleaned about an hour before closing. Jane stood across the street and watched the last customer leave the restaurant. Then she rushed into the building and went into a bathroom stall. She put her feet on the toilet to further hide her body.

However, Jane didn't know that Mandy, one of her co-workers, had seen her sneak in. Mandy was a double major in Chemistry and Biology as an undergraduate. She was very tech savvy and now taught online classes for the local university twice a week.

"What is she doing here? Isn't it her night off?" Mandy thought. Mandy clocked out of her shift then went to go look for Jane. She creeped into the bathroom and burst open the stall.

"Ahh," Jane screamed! "You scared me!"

"What are you doing here? Why are you hiding in the bathroom?" Mandy asked.

"What's it to you?" Jane fussed.

"You aren't supposed to be here. Are you trying to rob this place?" Mandy asked.

"No! Of course not," Jane said angrily.

"Well you better spill the beans right now or I'm telling," Mandy replied.

Immediately Jane hopped off the toilet and pushed Mandy up against the wall. She grabbed a fistful of Mandy's shirt.

"You better not tell my business or I'll beat your face in," Jane said.

"Okay. Okay. I won't but you are putting me in an awkward position. I don't want to be seen as your accomplice and lose my job," Mandy said.

"You won't--so leave!" Jane replied while un-gripping Mandy.

Mandy brushed off her shirt and said, "Fine. Suit yourself." Then headed towards the door.

At that moment, Jane immediately realized that maybe a better plan would be to crash at Mandy's place for the night so she humbled herself and changed her posture toward Mandy.

"Wait!" Jane said.

Mandy paused and faced Jane.

"I'm sorry. The truth is that I had a horrible day. I broke up with my boyfriend and I have nowhere to go," Jane stated.

"Is that it? Well ironically, I just put an ad out for a roommate. If you can pay $1800 a month then it's yours," Mandy stated.

"Ok. I can do that," Jane said.

"Well let's go. You can come check out my place and see if it interests you," Mandy said.

When the women got to the apartment, Mandy showed Jane around.

Jane nodded her head in approval. "I will take it. I'll get the money in the morning."

"Great. Well, here is your new room. Fresh towels are in the bathroom closet. Good night," Mandy said. Then she walked to her room and closed the door.

That night Jane laid across the bed and suddenly all the images of the day flooded her mind. Of all the things that could happen to a person in a single day. Get cheated on, becoming homeless, and see a random guy with pulsing green energy knock out and disable a bunch of people? This was truly unbelievable. She couldn't fathom Josh cheating on her and the weird man in the park.

"All those poor people," she said and began to sob. Jane drifted off into a deep sleep.

As she slept, she had a horrible nightmare. She dreamt that she was getting some ice cream and the man from the park followed her. While she was at the stand, he crept up behind her and tapped her on the shoulder. She turned and faced him but was horrified when she recognized his face.

"I got you," he said. Then he lifted up his arms, the sky darkened, lightning flashed, and green electricity came out of his body into hers. Jane dropped her ice cream and screamed. However, Jane didn't wake from the dream but tossed and turned in the bed while screaming, "Stop. Leave me alone," though still in a very deep sleep.

Down the hall, Mandy hears cries and gets up to check on Jane. When she entered the hall, she was seized by fear at the sight of the greenish glowing light shining underneath the door. However she didn't let her fear stop her. If Jane was in trouble she wanted to help. When she burst into Jane's room, she cut on the light and froze. Shock gripped her because she immediately saw the state of Jane.

Jane's skin appeared grey and she reminded her of the tin man from the Wizard of Oz. Green light was pouring out of Jane's mouth, ears, and the corners of her eyes.

"Jane! Wake up!" Mandy shouted in fear. She flew back, hit the wall, and slid down. After regaining herself, Mandy put her hand over her mouth, in sheer terror, to prevent herself from screaming.

At this moment, Jane sat straight up in bed. Her heart was racing and she was drenched in sweat. Coming to herself, Jane noticed that her skin was like lead again and she saw Mandy staring at her in disbelief in the corner.

"Oh no," Jane said. "Please don't think I'm crazy or kick me out. I don't understand what is going on with me or why these things are happening. Don't be afraid, please. I won't hurt you."

Trying to logically work through what she'd just seen, "Okay. I have never seen anything like this before. If you like I can try to run a few tests to see what's going on. I have a chemistry and biology degree. I teach multiple science classes for the university throughout the week," Mandy offered.

"Yeah. I would like that. All this started yesterday as I was drawn to go to the lab that burned down. When I stepped into the building, I tasted chemicals, my skin turned grey and my eyes glowed. It freaked me out so I decided not to pick up any extra shifts. Instead I went home and found my ex-boyfriend who I was living with in the bed with another woman," Jane explained.

"Oh you poor thing," Mandy sympathized.

"That's not all. After I caught my ex cheating, I went to the park to think and this weird guy came up to me with a note and money. The note had an address but I refused to help because it didn't seem right. Well the man went to someone else in the park asking for help and the lady took some of the money and handed the rest of it back. That made the man very angry. Suddenly, green energy came out of him and everyone in the park was paralyzed and pills started popping out of their skin. The pills went inside of the man's jacket and he took off. I was hiding behind the bench and wasn't affected at all. I called 911 to get the people help and went to the police station to report what I'd seen. They laughed at me."

"My. That is quite a fascinating story. By the sound of it, I believe you have some type of immunity to the green energy coming from the man," Mandy stated.

"You don't believe me do you?" Jane asked.

Mandy hesitated and said, "Well I need to do some investigating to process everything." She stood up.

"Wait! Look on the internet. You will see that I'm not lying. I was in the park on Lexington Avenue," Jane exclaimed.

The two women left the room and Mandy went and got her laptop. She did a web search and she saw a few news clips about it. She clicked on a video.

"Down in Lexington Park there are hundreds of bodies lying on the ground in some type of comatose condition. Here we have EMS on the scene working and providing critical care. If you know anything or have seen something please call the police depart-ment," the news reporter said.

"Wow. I believe you now. Maybe you are some kind of superhero in the making and I'm your side kick like Batman and Robin," Mandy joked.

"Oddly, I thought the same thing," Jane replied.

"Tell me about this man?" Mandy asked.

Jane began to explain in great detail and the two women came up with a plan. First, Jane would have her DNA analyzed. Next they would visit the burned down lab for clues. Lastly, they would track down this mysterious man so he wouldn't hurt anyone else. The two women said goodnight and headed back to their rooms.

The next morning, the two women sat down at the kitchen table and had the television playing. Suddenly, there was a breaking news report.

"Hello. I am Christy Jones and I'm standing out-side of Sunnyside Eggs And Grille. Apparently, there are multiple people inside in a comatose state. We have footage of the security camera and you can see a man wearing a trench coat with a fedora. It appears that this man is responsible for what we see here today. If you have any information about this man please call us at 1-888-590-3457 or the police department.”

Both of the women stared in shock. “That’s the man at the park,” Jane exclaimed. “Now the police should believe me.”

“Wait. I don’t think involving the police is such a good idea. They didn’t believe you the first time and you said that the man’s powers affected everyone except you. If you go back, they may target you or allow others to know about you. That may very well lead to others getting hurt, right?” Mandy asked.

“No. You’re right,” Jane stated. “Let’s go ahead and do what we agreed to do.” The two women dressed and left the apartment.

The first stop was the university lab. Jane provided a DNA sample for Mandy to examine later. As the two ladies exited the building, there was panic in the streets. People were screaming, crying, and running. A man was running towards them and they asked him, “What’s going on?” He yelled, “A bunch of people were hurt at the bank.” Then he continued to run.

"The bank is right around the corner," Mandy said.

"Oh no. I bet you it's that man," Jane replied.

The two women rushed towards the bank while others were rushing away from the bank. When they made their way inside, they saw everyone in a coma-tose state. The tellers were on the floor, the security was slumped over, and the customers were laid out overlapping each other like dominos.

"Yep, the mysterious man was here," Jane said. The two women left the bank and were on their way to the lab that got burned down. As they approached the building, Mandy noticed some of Jane's physical appearances were altering. Her skin started to turn an ashy grey and her eyes started to glow green.

"I can taste the chemicals in the air and I know the reason for this explosion was a nuclear reaction," Jane exclaimed.

"Wow. Your appearance has fully changed. I can't get too close to the site because it may not be safe for me but you can," Mandy said.

Jane went to go look around while Mandy stood at the fence barricade to keep watch. Jane squeezed between the opening and went inside the lab. Inside she found a notebook that was partially damaged. However she could see some of the writing. She kept seeing that the scientist's name was Dr. Oban. She took some pictures of the notebook with her phone and left the burnt building.

When she meets back up with Mandy she shares her discoveries. The further the two ladies walked away from the building, Jane's appearance normalized. When they got on the main street, the sound of ambulances were blaring as they whizzed by en route to the bank. They got on their phones to search for any news alert and saw that Dr. Oban put people who visited the movie theaters and the mall in a comatose state. One news report said, "Crime is increasing due to a mysterious ailment. Stay home."

Another news report said, "Hospitals are at maximum capacity because hundreds of people are in a comatose state."

"We've gotta stop this guy. The next stop is 511 Park Avenue," Jane said.

The two friends walked a short distance and approached the address. To their surprise, the address was an abandoned building. Jane opened up a lower level window and creeped in. Mandy followed. Adrenaline flowed through them both.

Inside the building were a few stretchers with straps. There was some lab equipment.

"Let's get out of here before he catches us," Mandy said.

"Yeah, good idea," Jane agreed.

The ladies came out through the window and ran from the building as quickly as they could.

"That was creepy," Mandy said.

"Yes," Jane replied. "I could taste some Chromium, Aluminum, and bromide in the atmosphere. Those are the same elements I tasted at the burnt lab. I could tell Dr. Oban has been there recently doing some experiments. We will get to the bottom of this and stop him."

CHAPTER 3

THE EXPLOSION

Dr. Oban was a highly esteemed chemist. He devoted his life to epidemiology and how it affected the indigenious population. Sometimes he worked from sun up to sun down even forgetting to eat. He was driven to find the cure for Xeno-19, a contagious flu that made people cough, lose an immense amount of weight and suffer chronic nose bleeds. He lost his sister Margaret, his only friend, to Xeno-19. Margaret truly understood him. When they were younger she would defend him when the other kids would pick on him.

One day, when Margaret was shopping with Dr. Oban, she put her hand on her forehead and paused pushing the cart. Dr. Oban looked at his sister.

"What is wrong?" he asked.

"I don't know," Margaret said. "I just don't feel good."

"Okay, sister. Go in the car, rest and I'll finish shopping here," he instructed. Margaret followed his advice and walked out to the car.

When he got in the car, he noticed that Margaret looked pale and her skin was clammy. He put his hand on her forehead and felt for himself that she was feverish. Dr. Oban took Margaret home, put her in the bed, gave her some Tylenol, and placed a glass of water on the nightstand. Margaret appeared weak and slept throughout the day.

A couple of hours later, he took her temperature again and she was still feverish. The next day, Dr. Oban took his sister to the hospital but the doctors did not know what was wrong with her. They ran multiple tests, drew labs, and performed a chest x-ray. The test showed that her white blood cell count was elevated but everything else was normal so they sent her back home.

Margaret didn't have much of an appetite and wouldn't eat. Dr. Oban had to force his sister to eat. Margaret would sip on tomato soup or chicken broth but after a few drinks, she stopped trying to receive nourishment because she couldn't stomach it. As a result, Margaret started to lose a massive amount of weight.

Out of nowhere Margaret's nose started to bleed and she had this horrible cough. Dr. Oban was very concerned about his sister so he took her back to the hospital. That night when he took her into the emergency room there was a doctor who had previously seen another patient with the same symptoms as Margaret. He was a traveling physician and practiced at different hospitals in the region and his expertise in infectious diseases was well recognized.

As Dr. Oban and Margaret were in their Triage room, the physician came and tapped lightly on the door. As he stepped into the room, he had a face shield and an isolation gown.

"I think you might have Xeno-19," the physician stated.

Dr. Oban and Margaret looked puzzled. They never heard about this disease before.

The physician could tell they lacked an understanding so he further explained.

"It's a contagious disease that makes you cough, lose weight, and have chronic nose bleeds. We have to keep this door closed to prevent the spread of the virus to other patients and staff. You have to wear a mask and quarantine until the symptoms resolve," he stated.

"How did I get this disease?" Margaret asked weakly. It took every ounce of strength she had to talk.

"Well, we believe this virus is associated with overseas trips, cruises, or plane travel. Have you been out of the country or took a trip recently?" the physician asked Margaret.

She nodded yes because her throat was coarse and very sore.

"Rest up. We will take care of you. I will write you some prescriptions for the fever and cough. We will continue to monitor you while you are here," the physician stated. He turned around and proceeded to walk out of the room but Dr. Oban stopped him.

"Doc, before you go? Do you think I'm affected by Xeno-19 since my sister and I are always in close proximity to one another and I am her caretaker?" Dr. Oban asked.

"Yes, but sometimes people don't show any symptoms. They are still very contagious," the physician stated. The physician exited the room.

Margaret and Dr. Oban stayed in the emergency room for a few more hours before she was discharged. Margaret was sent home with some antibiotics and something to ease her cough.

Early the next morning, Dr. Oban went to the local clinic and got tested for Xeno-19. Before he left, he made sure that Margaret had soup and water at her bedside. However, she was sound asleep. His test came back positive. Since he didn't have any symptoms, he was instructed to isolate himself to protect against spread.

Margaret declined quickly over the next few weeks, then she suddenly passed away. On the day of her death, Dr. Oban was cooking dinner. He was making a grilled steak and oversized baked potato for himself. For Margaret, he prepared some chicken noodle soup. When her soup was ready, he brought it to her room. He set the tray down on the nightstand.

"Hey, sis. Wake up. Let's get some liquids in you," he stated. He nudged Margaret but she was unresponsive. Dr. Oban nudged her again repeatedly but she didn't move. He checked to see if she was breathing and felt for a pulse and found none.

"Nooo!" Dr. Oban yelled. After alerting emergency services, having the technicians come over and remove Margaret's body, Dr. Oban settled into his grief. He wept bitterly throughout the night.

He was crushed because his sister was a huge part of his world. Who would listen to him now when he shared his life breaking research? Who would he spend time with on the weekends? He lost his best friend and Margaret was the only one who understood him.

A couple weeks after Margaret's death, Dr. Oban devoted more time than ever to the lab. He wasn't eating or sleeping properly. Dark circles began to appear underneath his eyes. Sometimes, he wouldn't shower because he didn't want to be away from his work.

One day while in the lab, he was experimenting with new chemicals but out of tiredness he made a few mistakes that proved fatal. He mixed a few chemicals that were explosive and, most importantly, radioactive. Dr. Oban got a flask, started mixing and then all of a sudden, a great combustion happened first hitting Dr. Oban in the face and then propelled him across the room. Glass shattered everywhere. A thick toxic smoke that burned the sinuses filled the room and the fire spread rapidly. The lab went up in flames but adrenaline coursed through Dr. Oban giving him the strength to make it out just in the nick of time.

Outside the building, Dr. Oban, exhausted and overwhelmed, collapsed on the ground outside of the building. He lay there for a few minutes before he opened up his eyes. When he looked at himself he noticed something strange. His hands were translucent almost as if he was invisible and there was green smoke coming out of his mouth.

He was so afraid that he ran to the first clothing shop that he saw. When he walked inside a lady immediately gasped and put her hand over her mouth because it looked like there should be a body wearing glasses but there was no body.

Dr. Oban panicked and snatched the first coat that he saw on the rack then he ran out the store. Now that he had a jacket on he could be seen. That was the start of Dr. Oban's transformation. Dr. Oban always considered himself an honest man but he justified his actions to steal due to his circumstances.

Over the next few weeks, Dr. Oban searched desperately for help. He needed to gain a greater understanding of what was wrong with him. He noticed that when he got upset, the sky would change, lightning would strike, and any medication or chemicals around him would float in the air then get sucked into his body.

He studied different reactions to try to discover how he had power over the elements. Dr. Oban needed an assistant or someone that he could perform clinical trials on. He needed to test their DNA so he could be cured. Dr. Oban had recently won a grant for his research a few months prior and he was willing to offer a willing participant a hefty price for their help.

One day in the park, he was looking around trying to find people. He gave them a note with his lab address, 511 Parker Ave, along with money. When he felt a young lady was taking advantage of him and people didn't want to help him, it infuriated him. His reaction caused darkness to fill the sky and lightning to strike all around him and green radioactive energy surged through his body. When people saw what was taking place, they started to run. However, it was too late. They were paralyzed on the ground and medication began to emerge from their skin and entered into his trench coat. This was the same day when Jane first saw Dr. Oban.

Overtime, Dr. Oban became frustrated and bitter in his heart because of his condition. He decided to no longer ask for help but to take the pills out of people's bodies himself. Once he collected the pills he went back to his lab. He extracted the pills out of his coat pocket and put them in tubes, funnels, flasks, and jars. He would break down the pills into different elements trying to find a cure for himself. Discovering a cure for Xeno-19 was no longer his priority.

Across the other side of the city, Jane and Mandy sat at the island in their apartment.

"Jane, you need to start training in order to beat this guy," Mandy said.

"Yes, you are right but how do I train?" Jane asked.

"Well you have to be physically fit so show me how many push-ups you can do?" Mandy inquired.

Jane got on the floor and proceeded to do push-ups but could only do five.

"Uggh," she said before falling over.

"Okay, we got work to do. How many sit ups can you do?" Mandy challenged.

Jane was still on the floor so she got into the sit up position and could not pass 20. She made a face because there was so much pain from not using those muscles in a while.

"Okay, enough. Let's go out to the park and see how fast you can run," stated Mandy.

When the two ladies got to the park, Jane began to do short sprints to build up her stamina. Mandy had her stopwatch on her cellphone and clocked Jane's speed at 5 minutes and 30 seconds.

"Okay, we definitely have to practice," Mandy stated.

Every day the women would work out and Mandy would record Jane's progress. Mandy would hold up a pillow for Jane to punch because they didn't have a punching bag to build up her strength.

Overtime Jane got faster and stronger. Jane made sure she drank protein shakes daily to build muscle. She was now able to do 100 sit ups in two minutes. She could now do 50 push-ups. The two ladies used monkey bars to build up her upper body strength. Jane was able to do 15 pull ups by the end of it all.

Mandy even clocked Jane's improved sprint at 1 minute and 30 seconds.

Now that Jane was in shape, her ability to taste needed to be tested. Jane could always taste chemicals and different elements in the atmosphere. So the two women began driving to different chemical plants. Jane would get out of the car and her body would react. Her skin turned gray and her eyes glowed. She was able to taste the petroleum, carbon, and the magnesium in the air.

Now that they knew she could taste, they wanted to see the length of distances she could go and still could taste the elements in the air. So they measured the distance between where the chemicals tasted the strongest to where she stopped tasting them. They decided to use the taste factor as a way to track Dr. Oban. Amazingly Jane was able to taste at least 50 km away. Mandy tracked Jane's progress in a notebook.

Most importantly, Mandy was determined to go to the lab and test Jane's DNA. When she put her DNA underneath the microscope she was shocked at what she discovered. Her cells were covered in a thick substance around the cellular wall. When she took a sample of the cell wall, she noticed that it had the components of lead and concrete.

Jane was immune to Dr. Oban's energy because her cellular DNA was strong enough to resist and stop him. Lead is known to stop radioactive decay, which Mandy discovered Dr. Oban's energy was derived from.

CHAPTER 4

THE DISCOVERY

After Mandy left the lab, she returned to her apartment. Jane was sitting on the couch and she explained her findings. Jane was shocked that her cells were made out of concrete and lead. She wondered how this was possible.

Jane and Mandy agreed that Jane was ready to confront Doctor Oban. The news reports kept coming in about Dr. Oban and this really annoyed them. He continued to put people in a comatose state. Jane grew angrier and vowed to stop him.

Around 9 o'clock that night, Dr. Oban was standing in front of an Italian restaurant. He was getting ready to strike again but at that moment Jane and Mandy pulled up in their car.

"Stop right there," Jane yelled as she hopped out of the vehicle.

Dr. Oban looked around to see who was speaking and when his eyes landed on Jane, he immediately recognized her.

"You," he said with an irritated fit. He was frustrated and didn't appreciate Jane interrupting him.

"Yes, it's me. Don't you touch another person," Jane shouted.

Dr. Oban was infuriated by her impudence. He raised his arms and the sky darkened. He tried to strike Jane with his radioactive power but missed. When he realized that he couldn't hit her, he rushed into her with the force of a linebacker. Jane flew back into the air and slammed into Mandy's car and instantly Dr. Oban disappeared into the night.

Mandy got out of the car, ran to help Jane, and brushed off debris. The impact dented the hood of the vehicle. Jane looked defeated and completely deflated.

"Do not give up because one defeat doesn't stop the victory," Mandy encouraged Jane.

"You're right," Jane replied.

Mandy's words resonated with her and motivated her to study Dr. Oban even more. She had to learn his tactics in order to defeat him successfully. When the two women got back to their apartment they went back to the drawing board.

"I noticed a pattern. Most of the attacks happened at night in a busy area. I believe he targets a mass of people at once," Mandy observed.

"True. I also noticed that he doesn't have any particular victims in mind when he strikes. He just attacks random people," Jane added.

Over the next few days, Jane kept picking up Dr. Oban's whereabouts through her exemplary senses. Each time she showed up where he was and confronted him.

"Dr. Oban, stop right there!" she yelled.

Dr. Oban would try to hit her with his radioactive power but he was always unsuccessful. He knew he couldn't beat Jane so he fled the scene each time. Because Jane was on the scene, many lives were saved. Jane took Dr. Oban's focus off the people and placed them on her. People began to thank Jane and got wind of her identity.

Later on that day, Mandy suggested for Jane to protect herself by concealing her identity. As a result, Mandy decided to make Jane a costume. It consisted of a black leather butterfly shaped mask, and a black body suit with blue stripes. She put a big blue T logo on the chest. When she was finished, she knocked on Jane's door and handed her the outfit. Jane looked surprised.

"Do you like it," Mandy asked.

"Wow. Yes. You went all out," Jane exclaimed.

"Good," Mandy smiled.

"What does the T stand for?" Jane inquired.

"T stands for Tabuletta. It's Latin for pills. You are a pill stopper," Mandy joked.

"Ha, ha. I love it," Jane chuckled.

Initially Jane thought it was corny but kept her thoughts to herself because she was grateful for Mandy's assistance.

"Let me try this on and I'll be right out," Jane stated. Mandy left and went into the living room. Jane hopped off her bed and put on the outfit. She loved the way it accentuated her curves. She felt like Catwoman. Jane put on some knee-high boots and did a spin in the mirror. She also put on some thick gloves that went up to her elbows so she wouldn't hurt her fist if she had to knock out her arch enemy.

"Oh my goodness. I look super fly!" Jane exclaimed. She walked out of the room to show Mandy. When she saw Jane, her mouth dropped open.

"Yes, we have a winner! You look the part now," she reassured her. The two women high fived each other.

Jane knew she was becoming a superhero and felt like she was ready to destroy Dr. Oban. It really bothered Jane that she had no idea why or how she got the powers. She needed answers so she decided to do some soul-searching and tried something she never did before. She went to a church, got on her knees, and prayed.

"Dear Lord, please reveal to me why I am like this. Amen."

She didn't know how to pray or the right words to say. All she knew was to speak what was in her heart. Jane got up and walked out to church. About three days later Jane began to have vivid dreams. As she slept, her skin was grey and her eyes glowed from underneath her eyelids.

In the dreams, she saw herself as a little girl lying in the hospital bed. She was pale and sickly. It seemed so real and she felt like she was right there while everything was occurring. She saw a man putting some medication in her IV.

Jane woke up from the dream but couldn't shake it. She knew that this must have happened when she was young. All of the hardships Jane faced caused her to suppress the bad memories. She started to remember as she reflected on the dream that as a child she was very sickly.

She wished she could call her parents but they were deceased. They died many years ago in a car accident. She knew she could not get answers from her parents so she prayed again.

"Dear Lord, thank you for showing me myself as a little girl. Please show me the answer that I'm seeking you for. What did the doctor put in my IV while I laid in the hospital bed?"

That night Jane went back to sleep and got the answer she prayed for. She dreamt about a man named Dr. Hyde. He was a renowned doctor who traveled to the Congo and the Amazon. He studied botany along with zoology and understood how the animal kingdom worked. His travels allowed him to interact with indigenous people and dangerous carnivores. Dr. Hyde was knowledgeable of different cultures with distinct customs and traditions, which may seem abnormal to a Western mindset.

While Dr. Hyde was in the Congo, he traveled to a shrine. Along the way he came across some strange plants that were the prettiest green he laid eyes upon. Each plant had a rich purple flower where the ovary and ovule were golden like honey. It was breathtaking. He wanted to know more about this mysterious plant along with its flowers so he took some and stuffed it in his pocket. However as soon as he touched the plant something happened to him.

He noticed that his fingertips started to immediately turn gray as a rock. He was frightened yet mesmerized. He wrapped his hand up with a handkerchief then headed towards the shrine. He didn't want anyone to notice it.

Once he got to his loft, he took a stone and ground it into a powder then placed it in vials. A couple of hours passed and his skin appeared normal. "Fascinating," he thought.

Overtime Dr. Hyde realized that he never got sick. He knew it was because of the plant. He expected to catch a cold because he usually became ill after traveling to different regions but month after month, he stayed in perfect health. He began to use the powder weekly and put a small amount of his palms. They would turn grey but normalize shortly after.

Once while traveling in the Amazon, some of his peers had food poisoning from eating undercooked Guinea pig. Dr. Hyde ate the same food and wasn't affected. He knew that it was due to this plant.

After his mission ended, Dr. Hyde came back to America and started writing research papers to submit to national publications. He wanted to share about his fascinating discovery. Dr. Hyde took up an internship at a hospital in his area. While he was there he heard some of his colleagues have a conversation about a poor little girl that was on the verge of death.

"Five year old Jane Walker is sickly and has been in and out of good health for months. We do not know what is wrong with her," the team of doctors said.

They had a board meeting about Jane's treatment plan, reviewed her tests, and came up with a course of action.

While his colleagues were in the board meeting, Dr. Hyde went into Jane's room and secretly injected some of the plant serum into Jane's IV line. He smiled as he inserted the medication and he exited the room. He knew that little Jane would pull through.

Twenty-four hours later, little Jane made a turn around. The board of doctors were puzzled and didn't understand why she recovered in such a miraculous manner. Some of them proclaimed that her recovery was a miracle. Jane's color came back along with her strength. She got her appetite back and was able to sit up in bed. Jane cried out to her parents.

"Mom and Dad, I'm ready to go home."

That was the last day Jane was ever sick again. Early that morning, Jane woke up from the dream and was thrilled that God finally answered her prayers. She rushed into the living room and found Mandy on the couch watching the news.

"It is getting worse. We have to stop Dr. Oban," Mandy stated.

"Yes. I think I'm ready now," Jane said. "I know how I got these powers and I know why my cellular DNA is like this. I prayed and God showed me that a man named Dr. Hyde put a serum in my IV when I was sick in the hospital room as a child."

Mandy was amazed at her succinct revelation.

"You have the strength to combat the radioactive waves of Dr. Oban. Since he is invisible, we have to make a specialized suit to contain his energy. The last time he rushed into the night and we couldn't see him. The suit will be made out of lead so we can trap him," Mandy proclaimed.

"Yeah- that's a great idea," Jane replied.

"This is how it will work: when you sense Dr. Oban in the atmosphere by tasting chemicals we will go to his location and confront him. As soon as we get visual of him, we will throw the lead suit on him and trap him," Mandy explained.

"Sounds like a good plan," Jane agreed.

"But where will we get this suit from?" Jane asked.

"Leave that to me," Mandy demanded.

Mandy spent the entire day working feverishly into the night developing a specialized suit for Dr. Oban. She even crafted a lead vest for herself because that's what x-ray technicians wear to stop radioactive decay. She wanted to ensure her own safety since she was called to help Jane takedown Dr. Oban. Secretly, she relished in being a super hero's sidekick, too!

CHAPTER 5

THE BATTLE

The next morning Mandy was exhausted from working throughout the night. She managed to doze off for a couple of hours but her sleep was interrupted when Jane tapped on her door.

"Come in," Mandy yawned while she was lying in bed.

"Wake up sleepy head. It's lunch time," Jane said as she stood at the entrance of the doorway.

"Oh no. It felt like I just went to bed," Mandy groaned as she put the pillow over her head and rolled over. She closed her eyes and proceeded to go back to sleep.

"Ok. I will leave you alone," Jane said. She was about to close Mandy's door but remembered the suit. "Hey, did you make the suit?"

"Yes. It's over there - lying on the ottoman," Mandy said.

Jane walked over to the ottoman and examined the lead suit. "Nice work. I can see you made something for you, too. You might as well get up. Come eat lunch with me and go back to bed. I'll go make you coffee and a salad. I know you are trying to watch your shape," Jane joked as she walked out the room and closed the door.

"Ha, ha, ha. You got jokes," Mandy replied. She was tired but she managed to get out of bed, shower, dress, and then head to the kitchen.

Jane had made a lovely lunch and the two started to eat. Suddenly out of nowhere, Jane threw the fork down on her plate and made a face of disgust.

"Yuck! I can taste him. That's a bad combination with salad in my mouth," Jane exclaimed.

"Really?" Mandy inquired.

"Yes, he's near. Let's get dressed quickly in our new suits and stop him before it's too late," Jane instructed.

The two women rushed, got ready, and jumped into the car. Mandy made sure she grabbed the lead suit for Dr. Oban. As Mandy drove, Jane instructed her where to turn based on the strength of her tastes sensing Dr. Oban's location.

"Turn down Lexington. Now make a right. He is right in this area," Jane said.

Mandy continued to drive slowly as they scoped out the surroundings. As they passed a jewelry shop, Jane yelled out.

"Make a u-turn. He's in there!" Jane said as she pointed to the jewelry shop.

Mandy whipped the car around and parked in front of the store. Jane got out of the car, rushed into the shop, and Dr. Oban was there preparing to strike again. When he heard the bells ring from the opened door, he looked up and saw Jane. He fled and took off through the back exit. Jane chased him but Dr. Oban removed his jacket so she couldn't see him. Jane went back into the store to check on the condition of the bystanders. They confirmed that they were alright.

Jane jumped back into the car and Mandy started to drive. Five minutes later while in travel, Jane started to taste that Dr. Oban was in the area.

"Okay. Pull over. Dr. Oban is near," Mandy parked in a community lot. Jane got out of the car and tasted him all the way to the bank.

Dr. Oban was in the process of sucking out medication from people's bodies. It looked like a horror scene. The tellers and customers were slain on the floor paralyzed. They were fully aware of their surroundings.

"I command you to stop," Jane yelled as she entered the bank. At that moment, some of the pills went back into the people's bodies. Dr. Oban took his hand and threw a radioactive wave at Jane but she was able to dodge it. He fled the scene again.

There were some outsiders standing on the street as Jane left the building. They were in awe of her costume and began recording her on social media and taking her photo. She managed to keep her cool and ran from the scene. Once she was out of sight, she texted Mandy her location, which was a food court.

"Finally I am at a place where I can get something to eat. I'm starving," Mandy said as she met Jane.

Jane got into the car and Mandy went inside and ordered them some stir-fry. Jane didn't want to draw attention to herself because of how she was dressed. Mandy wasn't wearing her lead vest that she had made so they agreed that she would get some food and they would eat it in the car. Mandy got some Hibachi and stir-fried vegetables. The two women devoured their lunch.

"I am tired of chasing Dr. Oban," Jane said.

"Me too," Mandy replied.

"Let's end this now!" Jane exclaimed.

"What do you propose?" Mandy asked.

"Let's go to 511 Park Avenue," Jane said.

"It could be dangerous," Mandy warned.

"Well we have to try. If we don't then how many people will get hurt?" Jane stated.

"You're right. Let's go!" Mandy said as she cranked the car up and drove off.

When the two women approached Dr. Oban's lab, they parked the car down the street. Mandy made sure to put on her vest and put the specialized suit for Dr. Oban in her bag. They quietly walked up to the building. Jane opened the old rusty door and tiptoed in. Meanwhile, Dr. Oban thought he heard someone coming. Upset at the many distractions from his plan on this day, he went to check it out. He walked down the hall and saw Jane and Mandy walking towards him.

They started running towards each other and the fight was on. Dr. Oban punched Jane in the stomach and she bent over in pain. Mandy kicked his leg and he yelled, "Ouch!" while turning around and slapping Mandy hard in her face. Mandy fell to the ground and was out for the count. Suddenly, Jane stood up and slammed Dr. Oban into the wall. He put his hands around her neck and started choking her.

Mandy saw her friend struggling so she looked at her surroundings. She saw a fire extinguisher hanging on the wall. She grabbed it and snuck up behind Dr. Oban. When she got closer to him, she smashed him over the head with it. He let go of Jane's throat and she was able to breathe. Dr. Oban passed out on the floor.

Jane started coughing while gasping for the air she lost.

"Quickly," Mandy said as she grabbed the suit out of her bag. "We have to put this on him now before he wakes up" she stated.

The two women sat Dr. Oban up and put the suit over his head and put his arms through it. Then they laid him back down. As they were laying him down, he woke up. The two women quickly contained him. Mandy sat on his feet while Jane sat on his chest. Mandy called 911 and they waited until the police arrived.

A few minutes later, the police arrived and the women explained everything. They revealed that Dr. Oban was the source of the attacks that were prevalent in the media. They instructed that he must keep on the specialized suit because it blocks his radioactive energy. One of the detectives asked Jane, "What is your name?"

She replied, "Call me Tabuletta."

Someone called for the detective's attention and he turned his for a quick moment. Yet when he turned back around, Mandy and Jane had left the scene. The detective tried to look for them but they were no-where to be found.

Later that day, a special holding cell was prepared for Dr. Oban. The walls were reinforced with concrete and lead paint was used. He was placed inside and the doors were secured. The only opening to the outside world was a little slot to slide a food tray through. The workers who got close to him were instructed to wear lead vests or they could be in danger of being para-lyzed. Dr. Oban was going stir crazy in his room. He began to talk and laugh to himself.

Meanwhile, some of the patients in the hospi-tal woke up out of the comatose state and were on their road to recovery. Jane, however, was a media sensation.

"They call her Tabuletta. Who is this mysterious woman?" the media inquired. They showed clips and photos of her that they gathered from social media. "Well Tabuletta, if you are watching, New York City thanks you for saving the day and putting the evil Dr. Oban away."

Mandy and Jane watched the news report together in their apartment.

"I hope it doesn't bother you that they are giving me credit. We both know who really took down Dr. Oban. I couldn't do this without you," Jane said.

"I know. I'm an asset," Mandy joked. "It doesn't bother me. I hate the spotlight. I would rather be in the background. I have horrible social anxiety. Together we will take down criminals."

"That's right," Jane stated. The two friends toasted a glass of sparkling apple cider and gobbled down some pizza.

ABOUT THE AUTHOR

Kimberly Moses started off her ministry as Kimberly Hargraves. She is highly sought after as a prophetic voice, intercessor and prolific author. There is no doubt that she has a global mandate on her life to serve the nations of the world by spreading the Gospel of Jesus Christ. She has a quickly expanding worldwide healing and deliverance ministry. Kimberly Moses wears many hats to fulfill the call God has placed on her life as an entrepreneur over several businesses including her own personal brand Rejoice Essentials which promotes the Gospel of Jesus Christ.

She also serves as a life coach and mentor to many women. She is also the loving mother of two wonderful children. She is married to Tron. Kimberly has dedicated her life to the work of ministry and to serve others under the call God has placed over her life. Kimberly currently resides in South Carolina.

She is a very anointed woman of God who signs, miracles and wonders follow. The miraculous and incessant testimonies attributed to her ministry are incalculable, with many reporting physical and mental healing, financial breakthroughs, debt cancellations and other favorable outcomes. She is known across the globe as a servant who truly labors on behalf of God's people through intercession.

She is the author of The Following:

"Overcoming Difficult Life Experiences with Scriptures and Prayers"
"Overcoming Emotions with Prayers"
"Daily Prayers That Bring Changes"
"In Right Standing,"
"Obedience Is Key,"
"Prayers That Break The Yoke Of The Enemy: A Book Of Declarations,"
"Prayers That Demolish Demonic Strongholds: A Book Of Declarations,"
"Work Smarter. Not Harder. A Book Of Declarations For The Workforce,"
"Set The Captives Free: A Book Of Deliverance."
"Pray More Challenge"

"Walk By Faith: A Daily Devotional"
"Empowering The New Me: Fifty Tips To Becoming A Godly Woman"
"School of the Prophets: A Curriculum For Success"
"8 Keys To Accessing The Supernatural"
"Conquering The Mind: A Daily Devotional"
"Enhancing The Prophetic In You"
"The ABCs of The Prophetic: Prophetic Characteristics"
"Wisdom Is The Principal Thing: A Daily Devotional"
"It Cost Me Everything"
"The Making Of A Prophet: Women Walking in Prophetic Destiny"
"The Art of Meditation: A Daily Devotional"
"Warfare Strategies: Biblical Weapons"
"Becoming A Better You"
"I Almost Died"
"The Pastor's Secret: The D.L. Series"
"June Bug The Busy Bee: The Gamer"
"June Bug The Busy Bee: The Bully"
"The Weary Prophet: Providing Practical Steps For Restoration"
"The Insignificant Woman"
"The Foolish Woman: A Daily Devotional"
"June Bug The Busy Bee: Sibling Rivalry"
"All Things Relationships"
"30 Day Pray For Your Spouse Challenge"
"The Christian Drama Queen Mentality"

"30 Days Praying For The Nations"
"Intercessor's Prayer Notebook"
"Prayer Request Notebook Fervent Effectual Prayers Of The Righteous"
"The Prophet's Notebook"
"The Photographer's Assistant"
"The Ultimate Entrepreneur"
"Diabetic Caretaker Blood Sugar Log"
"The Preacher's Handbook"
"Christian Weight Loss Journal"
"Couple's Recipe Meal Planner And Notebook"
"Prophetic Dreams And Visions Journal"
"The Therapist Secret: The D.L. Series"

You can find more about Kimberly at
www.kimberlyhargraves.com

For Rejoice Essential Magazine, visit
www.rejoiceessential.com

For beauty, hair, and t-shirts, visit
www.rejoicingbeauty.com

Please write a review for my books on Amazon.com

Support this ministry:
Cashapp: $ProphetKimberlyMoses
Paypal.me/remag

Venmo: Kimberly-Moses-19

Follow my YouTube Channels:
Kimberly Moses
Kimberly Finds